Books for B oys

The Fish that
Ate Me

By

Mr. Yee!

My books are a project to get my son to
enjoy reading. The stories use early
reading words and subject matter young
boys like. The words in the book range
from pre-primer through third grade words.
Early readers will find reading and learning
more enjoyable because of the appropriate
and interesting content.

For all boys who find reading boring!

Making Reading Fun!

ISBN 978-1-304-00260-0

The Fish that
Ate Me

Spring time means only one thing to me. Fishing! Flowers start to grow, but so do the fish! And big they grow!

Last summer I saw the biggest fish jumping out of the water. It was down by my favorite fishing spot.

Today I need to find my fishing pole and get my fishing box together.

First, I clean my pole. Next, I will open the reel and clean the gears.

I think I could catch the big one on this hook. "Ouch!" The hook cut my finger. "That hurt!"

I had better use the fly hook I made to try to catch the big one. The fly hook is yellow.

"Look!" The hook is red from the cut on my finger. I laugh at myself and pick up my pole.

Splash! I see the water move
to my right.

Splash! I turn around and look under the big brown tree. Splash! Again I see a big round of water splashes.

I will try to cast my fly by the round circle of water. My cast is long and lands next to the splash.

I let my fly go under the water and fall to the bottom. I hold tightly to my pole. "Please, please, please take the fly."

The fish bit my fly!

It was just after the sun had set. All that was left on that spring day was a long pole with a fly at the end of the line.

Some say they still see big round splashes under that brown tree.

The End

Keep Reading!

More Books from Mr. 7 Yea!

The Hunter
Cowboy
Fire Fighter
Runaway Sailboat
Cool Forts
Lost Campers
Baseball Wars
Dinosaurs
My Rocket Ship